D1195124

WHILE I STILL AM

A Story About Endangered Animals

Written and illustrated by Jodie A. Cooper

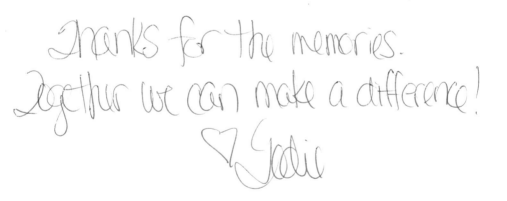

Thanks for the memories.
Together we can make a difference!
♡ Jodie

Published by
Hybrid Global Publishing
301 East 57th Street
4th Floor
New York, NY 10022

Manufactured in the United States of America, or in the United Kingdom when distributed elsewhere.

Cooper, Jodie
  While I Still Am: A Story about Endangered Animals
  LCCN: 2020911623
  ISBN: 978-1-951943-28-8

Cover design by: Jonathan Pleska
Interior design by: Claudia Volkman
Author photo by: Keith C. Saylor
Illustrations by: Jodie Cooper
Copyediting by: Erika Cooper

Every animal featured in this book
is on the endangered spectrum.
My hope is by teaching our children
compassion and how we can make
a difference in the world, these magnificent
creatures will remain for many generations.

This book is dedicated to Mini Cooper.
Love you to the moon and back!

We can judge the heart of a man by his treatment of animals.

IMMANUEL KANT

*If you think you're too small to make a difference,
try sleeping with a mosquito.*

DALAI LAMA

The love for all living creatures is the most noble attribute of man.

CHARLES DARWIN

I am an African Elephant. You can find me throughout the savannas of sub-Saharan Africa and the rainforests of Central and West Africa. I live in a female-led herd. I am a majestic animal who can live up to 70 years, grow to be 8-13 feet tall, and weigh 2.5 to 7 tons! My trunk can grow up to 7 feet long. Did you know I flap my large ears to keep me cool? Climate change and land development destroy my habitat. Poachers want my tusks to sell in ivory trade. I am hunted for big game thrill. I am captured to perform in circuses and for rides. Please leave me be while I still am.

I am a Mountain Gorilla living on the volcanic slopes of Uganda, Rwanda, and the Congo. I live in a pack of about 30 led by a dominant, older male. I am very intelligent and can be taught sign language. I can live up to 35 years, grow 4-6 feet in height, and weigh up to 300-485 pounds! I can climb, but you'll usually find me on the ground. I eat roots, fruit, and tree bark. Did you know I can stand up and walk on my back legs? I have a fierce voice that I use when I am threatened. Farming and forest production destroy my habitat. Climate change, human diseases, and traps are a threat to me. Please leave me be while I still am.

I am an African Lion. I am the "King of the Jungle" found in sub-Saharan Africa. I live in a pride of as many as 40 lions. I can live 10-14 years, grow to be 4-6 feet long, and weigh 265-420 pounds! Males have a beautiful head of hair called a mane. Lionesses in the pride are all related and are the hunters. They roam up to 100 square miles a day. Males defend the pride.

Did you know my roar can be heard for up to 5 miles away? Most of my threats come from humans who encroach my habitat for farmland, poison me to keep me away from their farm animals, hunt me for trophies, and poachers who sell my body parts in illegal trade. Please leave me be while I still am.

I am a Black Rhinoceros found sparsely in sub-Saharan Africa. Although I am known as a black rhino, I am actually gray. I can live 35-50 years, grow 4.5-6 feet tall at shoulder height, and weigh 1750-3000 pounds! I browse the land, plucking fruit from trees and bushes at night, dusk, and dawn with my pointed lip. During the day you will find me lying in the shade or wallowing in the mud. I have great hearing and sense of smell. Did you know my two horns can grow up to 5 feet long? I use them for protection. My only natural predator is man. I am hunted by poachers solely for my horns, which have no medicinal value.

Please leave me be while I still am.

I am a giraffe found in East and Southwest Africa. I live mostly in the Savannas in herds of 40 or so females and calves. I am the tallest mammal in the world, reaching heights of 14-19 feet. My legs alone are 6 feet long. I can live 25 years and weigh 1750-2800 pounds! I use my 21-inch tongue to pluck food from tree branches. Acacia trees are my favorite. I regurgitate my food and chew it as cud. Did you know that I give birth standing up? I can gallop at speeds of 35 miles an hour. I have a heart that weighs 25 pounds and is 2 feet long! I am gentle, posing no threat to man or animal. My coat has beautiful patterns and no two of us are alike. I am hunted as a trophy and by poachers for my hide and tail. Please leave me be while I still am.

I am a Grevy's Zebra. I am found in Ethiopia and Northern Kenya. I can live 22-30 years, grow 4-5 feet tall, 7 feet long, and weigh 750-1000 pounds! I am larger than other zebra species, my belly is mostly white, my ears are larger, and my stripes are narrower. Did you know my stripes are as unique as a human fingerprint? You will find me mostly in small female herds eating the rough tops of grass. I can go 4-5 days without a sip of water. I need large grasslands to survive. My habitat continues to be destroyed by grazing farm animals, and I am threatened by the diseases carried by livestock. I am also hunted for my gorgeous skin and for meat. Please leave me be while I still am.

I am a green sea turtle found in tropical and subtropical coastal waters. I can live to 80 years, grow up to 5 feet in length, and weigh up to 700 pounds! You can tell me apart from other sea turtles because I have a single scale in front of my eyes. I have flippers with claws so I can move quickly in the water. As a youngster, I eat fish and crustaceans. As an adult, I eat sea grass and algae. Did you know females migrate to lay their eggs, often on the same beaches where they were hatched? They will dig a pit in the sand, laying 100-200 eggs. My eggs are stolen for food, and many hatchlings never make it to the water as they are easy prey. In the waters, I get snared and die in shrimp nets. I am hunted for meat, leather, and as a trophy. Please leave me be while I still am.

I am an orca, sometimes called a "killer whale." Did you know I am not a whale at all? I am the largest of the dolphin species. I can be found swimming in cold coastal and polar equator waters. I can live 50-80 years, grow 23-32 feet long, and weigh up to 6 tons! I swim in pods of tight-knit family groups of up to 40, around 40 miles a day, diving from 100-500 feet. I feed on fish or marine animals and my pod hunts cooperatively. My pod has distinctive communication that helps us recognize each other. I am often slaughtered by illegal whaling vessels. I am very intelligent, and trainable, which is why I am also captured and sold to marine parks for entertainment. As I am a very social animal, I do not thrive in captivity. In captivity, I cannot swim and dive freely, so my dorsal fin collapses. Due to boredom and stress, I develop repetitive behaviors that cause harm to myself and others.

Please leave me be while I still am.

I am a hippopotamus, called a "river horse" by the Greeks. I am found in Eastern, Central and South sub-Saharan Africa. I can live up to 40 years, grow 9-14 feet long, weigh 1.5-4 tons, with a tail up to 19 inches long! I spend up to 16 hours each day submerged in water to stay cool. Did you know I am a good swimmer and can hold my breath for up to 5 minutes? Since my nostrils and eyes are high on my head, I can easily see and breathe while the rest of me is underwater. I usually feed at night, grazing many pounds of grass while walking several miles. When my calf is born, she can nurse underwater by closing her ears and nostrils. When I lie in the sun, I secrete a substance that acts as a sunblock and moisturizer. Logging and human settlement destroy my habitat. I am hunted for the ivory of my teeth, for meat, and for my skin. Please leave me be while I still am.

I am a Magellanic Penguin, named after the explorer whose expedition discovered me in the early 1500s. I can live 10-20 years, stand 24-30 inches tall, weigh 8-14 lbs, and have oily feathers that protect me against the cold waters. I am found on both the Atlantic and Pacific sides of Southern South America. Known for my black body and white belly, I blend in with the ocean. Did you know I mate for life and return to the same place I was born to nest? Both mom and dad raise the chicks. I eat small fish and migrate to Northern South America for the winter. My body is built for swimming, as I have webbed feet and long flippers. My habitat is threatened by climate change causing heavy rains that flood my nesting areas. I get caught and drown in fishery nets. Chronic oil pollution from ocean tankers remains my greatest threat. Please leave me be while I still am.

I am a Beluga Whale found in the Arctic and sub-Arctic coastal waters. I can live 35-50 years, grow from 13-20 feet in length, and weigh 1-1.5 tons! I am the smallest of the whales, with no dorsal fin and a distinct head. I live in a small group pod. I am very social and vocal. I am called the "canary of the sea" because I can whistle, clang, and click as well as mimic other sounds. I feed on fish, crustaceans, and worms. My calves are born gray or brown and don't turn white in color until around 5 years old. Did you know I can turn my head in all directions? I am threatened by climate change, and hunted by commercial fisheries and Northern people.

Please leave me be while I still am.

I am a Koala. Although I am called a Koala "bear," I am actually a marsupial, with a pouch for raising offspring. I can live up to 20 years, grow 23-33 inches tall, and weigh 20 lbs! You will find me in the eucalyptus forests of Southeast and Eastern Australia. The eucalyptus tree is both food and home for me. I eat a pound of eucalyptus a day. Did you know that the eucalyptus is toxic, so I have work hard to extract the nutrients during digestion? This is why I sleep so much. I climb trees and cling to them with my opposing thumbs, rough pads, and claws. I use my fused toes to comb my coarse, wool-like fur. Climate change increases carbon dioxide which decreases the nutrition of my eucalyptus leaves. My woodland habitat is shrinking from logging and forest fires.

Please leave me be while I still am.

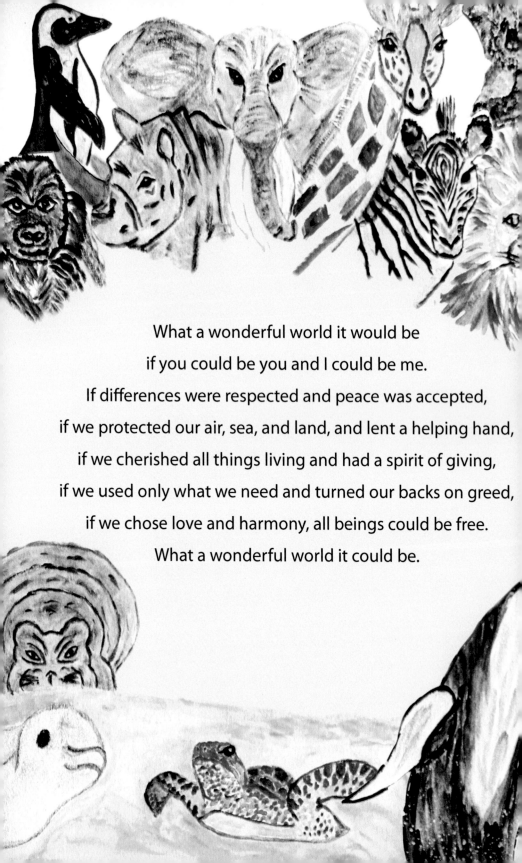

What a wonderful world it would be
if you could be you and I could be me.
If differences were respected and peace was accepted,
if we protected our air, sea, and land, and lent a helping hand,
if we cherished all things living and had a spirit of giving,
if we used only what we need and turned our backs on greed,
if we chose love and harmony, all beings could be free.
What a wonderful world it could be.

What can you do to help save the animals?

Protect the environment by using eco friendly products, recycle, and don't pollute. Learn as much as possible and support credible wildlife organizations in any way you can.

Animal Defenders International (https://www.ad-international.org)
African Wildlife Fund (https://www.awf.org)
Climate Change (https://www.globalchange.gov)
One Green Planet (https://www.onegreenplanet.org)
The Ellen Degeneres Wildlife Fund (https://www.theellenfund.org)
Wildlife Conservation Society (https://www.wcs.org)

Your neighborhood animal shelter can always use help!

Will these trophies be all we have left someday,
tokens of a wild nature we once knew?

MICHAEL PATERNITI, *NATIONAL GEOGRAPHIC*

What right do we have to do nothing about it?

SHELTER TO HOME, WYANDOTTE, MICHIGAN, USA

A true conservationist is a man who knows that the world is
not given by his fathers, but borrowed from his children.

JOHN JAMES AUDUBON

A portion of the proceeds from the sale of this book
will be donated to the groups listed here.

Acknowledgments

To Gerry for your unfailing love and support.

To Erika for editing, for being my constant sounding board, and for being you.

To Keith C. Saylor for your digital mastery.

To Karen Strauss for making my dream a reality.

To Soul Camp Creative for your wisdom and encouragement—WOOSH!